BELOW THE BELT
Suck-her Punch!

Purpose
Denise Cherubini
Jacki King
Mocha Mama
Maria James-Thiaw
The Priestess
T.L. Waid

Editing by Carla Christopher-Waid with
Missi Ritter
Graphic Design, Layout and Cover by
Carla Christopher-Waid
Printed in the United States for
PoemSugar Press
York, PA   www.poemsugarpress.com

ISBN-13: 978-0692380789
ISBN-10: 0692380787

3

BELOW THE BELT
Suck-her Punch!

PoemSugar Press
York, PA

What's Inside...

Purpose

Come Here

I want you to run my bath water
Get my soap
Light the candles and dim the lights
Baby, turn the slow music on
You are a spectator tonight
Tonight I want to please you
by pleasing me -
slowly touching and caressing
every one of my spots
See me
touch me
flawless

Mirrors cloudy ... tempers high
From my neck to my breast
over my stomach
my fingers slip in between my thighs
Your eyes
on my hands as I
move them to the song
My eyes closed, my head back
I moan as if I was alone
Taking my time
I watch you play with yours
as I continue to play with mine
and this bubble has got my wet
all over

This feeling so good
that I don't want it to be over
but my legs start to shake
the hot water vibrates
the inside of my thighs
tense up as my finger rides
my pussy

I can't wait
my legs
open
I need
to feel you inside me

Come here

Come Again

The foreplay was amazing but

sometimes I just want to be fucked
Hair pulled
Ass smacked
Choked
Bonded
Blind folded
and handcuffed
Once and a while I need it rough

I want you to touch it right there,
kiss it here
Yes, just like that

You know my favorite position baby
Take it from the back

Yes, make me scream your name
like I am your number one fan
Damn

I definitely want the dick but
I don't want it from a man

Ladies

Ladies,
have you ever prayed
for the perfect woman?
She would never hurt you
and you would feel secure in her hands
She is your fortress from the world
From the way she looks at you
you know you are her only girl
She is all your dreams come true
Your every prayer answered
She makes you feel
there can be a happily ever after

Yea, I prayed that prayer too,
but did you ever think to stop
and consider you?
Take a long look in the mirror
to evaluate what YOU
could bring to the table
Would you be able to have her
like she has you?
Not just financially
but spiritually
mentally
and emotionally too

As women we are so quick to judge
Does she have a car?

A job?
What is her income?
And all along were throwing stones
living in a glass house

So often we bring our old baggage
into our new home,
blaming her
for our insecurities
looking to her
for validation

Ladies,
the next time you pray,
make sure you're the perfect women
for your perfect girl

Denise

The First Kiss

Last night
When it seemed that your touch
Could heal
That aching flesh
That is my body
It seemed
That heaven had reached me
Erased the bitterness inside.
I felt, your spirit
Like flames
Licking at my spine
Wrapping itself up
Inside my mind.
And when, in your words
Not your caresses
Only he could have you
I sought that bitterness again
Or maybe, perhaps it sought me
Though I resisted.
The way angels do
When darkness descends
Upon fallen Kings & Queens
In a drunken palace
Made of steel.

Oh, that first kiss
Were I to have it again
The World would fall away.

What is this Earth?
Beneath my feet.
Is not the spirit, me?

Spring Dream Awakening

Spring dream
Awakening
I want
A beautiful flower
Opening up to me
Inner seed on fire
Revealing secrets
Sanctum bleeding

Water doused
Moist fruit
Blossom unfolding
Nectar juice.

Fuck Softly

I lie within the shallows
Of your heart
Your beginnings
Icy reservations &
Dry promises to sweat
Through & crawl & claw
& Call
I breathe fuck softly
& Slowly while you
Swear you never could
Fit a fist
I fit it in
Your cunt &
My anus
Bleeds
Softly
As you
Do the same
To it

I cry, "Yes.
Yes."
You say, "Tears are okay."
I beg, "Oh God."
You say, "Don't stop."
& We go on
All night

Thinking, this feeling
Will never end

And tears
Dry.

Crickets

Manifestation
Movements
Bright euphoric
Energies
Emanating alluring
Moon song of insects

Brisk sharp
Pulsing sounds
Dancing Women
Beckoning
Ritualistic
Rhythmic

Cricket legs
Scraping
Sliding
Vagina song of Crickets

In the savage Moonlight
Orgiastic Orthopterans
Rubbing their fleshy wings
Together
Different texture

Hairs dancing
Between the folds
Of sheets and flesh

Of flesh and sheets
Deep, into the
Moonlight
And early Morning
Sunrise,

We sing.

Cyber Zombie Drag King

Sulking skull and crazy cranium
Black helmet rising from hellish nest
Born of metal and mesh
w/plenty of volts & bolts to go around

Vampiric cape & electronic eye
Goggled drag god dragged raged & ragged
Skulking about tombstone death &
Mirrored mesh of bones and flesh
Eerie electronic instrument

Horror singing its eerie song of torture
From fetid landscape to smoky red sky
Apple orchard of the mind
Is it the apocalypse?
Is everyone going to die?

No, just the Cyber S&M Fetish drag guy.
Confusing everybody conservative but you.
You understand conceptualized drag king
performance poetry, don't you?
Electronic gender bender
evangelical love hound
He's the karaoke king
screaming beat poetry sound
He's the careening king of androgyny
A metallic monstrosity crowned

Plastic body with wires for hair
Industrial rag doll girl toy bound
Wearing men's underwear.
Mechanical tomboy
Dionysian angelic feast
A sexy super beast

By Goddess's grace
Metatron knows her place
Glamour boy dyke drag king
Mechanical man w/leather skin
Grab his joystick, play a game
Push a button, grab the controls
There's role-playing fun for everyone!

Embrace electricity macho
mechanical unctuosity
A melding of man, woman & machine
Computerized androgyny doll of tin
Highly interactive zombified
Computerized love creature thing
Created only for pleasure and no purpose
Drag boy love slave of steel
He cannot feel
Strutting about showing his stuff

Jacki

Cross My Heart

When I asked him about his day, he shrugged.

"I don't want to bore you," he said.

"I wanna know," I said. "Cross my heart."

But he didn't say a word.

When he fucked me, he fucked me from the side.

"I don't want to hurt you," he said.

"I'm heavy."

"But I want to feel your weight," I said.

"Cross my heart."

He fucked me from the side anyway.

When I was leaving, I put a note on the fridge.

"Your something will never crush me

the way your nothing does."

Cupid in Retrograde
(for Dave)

I don't know when my planets fell out of
line.

I don't remember moving them.

They took off on their own

Didn't even send me a change of address
card.

I don't recall what my horoscope said

The day I met you.

I remember telling you I'm a writer,

And you said you don't read

And I thought, "Honey, move on.

This ain't never gonna last.

Your Cupid's gone Retrograde."

But you were so cute

And I loved your blue eyes.

31

The first time you told me you would wash my car.

It was thirty degrees outside!

All you had was a bucket and a sponge.

I watched you squat down

Chisel away a gazillion specks of dirt.

You rinsed it all clean

Dried it with a diaper.

With every pat you put another planet back in place.

You knew where they were even when I didn't.

And I thought, "Honey, don't let this one go.

Your Cupid's gone Supernova."

Slut Shaming

If I love a man, I fuck him.
That's the way it's meant to be.
But you say I'm a slut.
If you love a man, you demand a diamond
A kid
A house
A dog.
Once, I gave a two-hour blowjob
On a Saturday morning
Just to see if I could do it.
Just 'cuz it was his favorite.
Once, you gave a two-minute bj
During the commercial break
Because you had to.
"It was his birthday."
Then, you made him take out the trash,
Told him to go mow the lawn.
When he was done, you said,
"Not tonight. I have a headache."
You nagged while he sat on the couch,
his eyes glazed over
Caring more about men
who play with one another
Than he cared about you.
Now, you wanna cry 'cuz he cheated.
"He made a promise," you whine,
Forgetting that you made one, too.
And you broke yours

long before he broke his.
No, I've never been married.
Never traded my body for a two-car garage
that buried us both
I trade my body for a feel-good moment
that makes my soul sing.
And the truth is,
diamonds don't make dicks hard.

Mocha

HE

Smellin' like Armani
with his body up against me
Tongues locked
Eyes closed
In this moment he has convinced me
that I was created just for him
and he just for me
As we intertwine our bodies and minds
so perfectly;
our chemistry goes soul deep
What we have gets hotter
than the fire's heat
I hang on to every word he speaks
To hear his voice,
to look in his eyes
makes my knees weak.

The passion we share,
how we move together without fear
the way we turn off the nonsense
and drop a deaf ear
represents something so rare
All truth
No dare.

His security
His personality
The way he brushes his hair

has convinced me
that I was created just for him
and he just for me
because he opened me up
He set me free
and I can't imagine living this life
without inhaling the air he breaths.

Tie Me Up

Blindfold me
Put your hands around my neck and
gently choke me
Bite me
Spank me
Yank my clothes off me
Whisper in my ear and kiss my body
from my chin
to my hips
to my lily
Fuck me silly
Let them hear me scream your name
from Harrisburg to Philly!

BLUEPRINT

Boooy! You don't know what I'll do to you
I'll have you under my hypnosis
by the way I move
Balls so blue you can't find your cool
because this feeling I give you
is beyond radical

Foolin' with me
will have you down on one knee

Oh you didn't know?
You better ask somebody
I am the blueprint
No carbon copy
Rock hard from the very thought of me
with my brown eyes
thighs wide
I gotchu you droolin' on yourself
all mesmerized.

Throat dry
Heart throbbin'
Once I get started
baby there's no stoppin'

Eyes closed,
breathin' heavy through your nose
Giving me full control

If I get too rough baby,
please forgive me
I just know you love it
every time I fuck your mind
before I even touch your body

Maria

The Connoisseur

The ping, ping, ping of
buttons hit the floor.
Bare breasts against your chest
melt into you;
When your cork pops,
I open, taste, swish you
around my mouth,
let you dance on my tongue;
Savor you
like sweet wine

Harlem Moon

                                I want
                            the moon
                        to slip on her
                    little black dress,
                    come out with me,
            and make the night shine.
        I'm tired of using televised
        voices to drown out the si-
    lence. The moon knows what I
    mean. The sun never sticks around
    long enough to keep her company. I
    want to step out despite the sounds
    of sirens, stray cat cries, woman-
        bashing bass beats and thug
        cursing. Let's go somewhere
            where I can close my eyes and
            dream of an earlier time when
                midnight-skinned men loved
                and could wring pleasure
                from a woman until it
                    spilled out of
                        her like
                            rain.

* (originally published in Talking "White," postDada press 2013)

Color Struck

There is power in this:

I paint hieroglyphics in oil-
turquoise and gold winged Isis
loving her Osiris,
ready to build nations
on the curve of his back.

My hands follow the pleasure in his voice,
knead his skin like dark clay—
we are caramel to chocolate
lavender to purple
morning to midnight.

My hand is the color of sunrise
over a dark ocean.
My fingers, the stars,
cross the moonlit night
between his shoulder blades.

A goddess, his joy in my palm.

* (originally published in Talking "White" by postDada press, 2013)

Priestess

Since You Asked...

I say your name
like a branding,
a testament to your ownership
in that moment

Your desire is
still cloaked in dusk and a
two drink minimum

crowded at small bistro tables
with a third
who whispers in your ear
he can feel how much I want you

You can feel my hand
riding the ridge of the butterfly wings
that flutter with your pulse
your desire
your worst kept secret

I seduce you
because your heartbeat
begs me to

Diner Late Night

You doodle with Sharpie on the sensitive
inner curve of my wrist, possessed of a
desire to mark me in ways more
permanent than the cherry glazed
kisses you drizzled with deliberate
slowness on the mounded cream of
coconut scented breasts.

You lips rest in the tender nook of inverted
elbow, the exact place an arm bends to
cradle and hold.

I do not push you away. It is my pleasure
to wear you like jewelry, who's beauty
enhances what loveliness I am fortunate
enough to contain.

8 Days Straight

Day 1   Straddling your desk chair, knuckle grip scratching fabric gray as the iron bridge riding the Susquehanna shores.

Day 2   My back arched over a river of sliding blue sheet. 600 thread count. It makes a difference.

Day 3   Ice blocking the window blinds left open for the cat to look out into the street, two melted palm prints and a half-formed O still steaming against the glass. The man next door particularly friendly the next morning.

Day 4   There is no metaphor for that you put the cowboy porn in the DVD player after dinner, during the time clearly marked "bill paying" in Google calendar.

Day 5   I read you poetry. I began to move as poetry. I began to feel like the damp spasming insides of a poem just about to reach its climactic line. You told me to allow my eyes to close, that you would finish the poem for me.

Day 6   The toy drawer. Fresh batteries.

Day 7   You peeled back the cover and found the leopard print stilettos, thigh highs and dual black Xs of heavy tape where nipples should be. I sweat them off.

Day 8   You held me. It's good to be married. You know I'll still be here tomorrow.

T. L.

The Fall of a Catholic Schoolgirl

I write poems
across your body with my tongue
brand your skin with my love,
purple bruises left behind as evidence

and make you my own

fuck you so well and so hard
that you forget
everything your mother taught you
about how to be proper and nice

There is nothing proper about you
in the dark of my bedroom

On your back,
your hips rise up to meet me
On your knees,
your ass begs to spanked

You plead for more

I push into you
Back arches
Legs spread

Wider

Deeper I push

Deep enough
to make the names of past lovers
lose all meaning
Deep enough
to make you forget even the most
rigid of Catholic school morals
Deep enough
to make you
cum
cum
and cum
some more

and then I do it all again

Hearing Aid

You left your hearing aid in tonight
Signed that you wanted to hear my
"Love sounds"
My ASL is poor to say the least
but when you go slow,
I catch every word
I understood your
"Make it loud baby"
in the middle of making love
Your monotone slowly says my name
I love it when you speak out loud
Your self-consciousness
makes it a rarity
I love your voice
To me it sounds like
hushed words of passion
The ones that when the shit is really hot
you can barely get out
Every sound you make
I feel like it is only for me
and when we are making love
I keep my promise to you
My moans and screams echo off
bare bedroom walls
I imagine your fingers inside of me
spelling out
Love
with each thrust

Su Ling

It was Friday night. My shift at the factory had run late and I was feeling kinda hungry, so I decided to dip down to my favorite Chinese restaurant. It was getting late and I knew they wouldn't be open much longer. The only food you could count on late night in the hood was Chinese and overpriced pizza.

Got there with half an hour to spare till closing. My favorite hostess greeted me with a smile.

"It is very late to see you tonight Trey. Do you want your usual?"

I had been comin' here to the Golden Dragon for months, ever since I moved from Maryland. One I hate to cook and two mostly because of Su Ling. The girl was hot. Like Jiffy Pop right off the stove hot. She had a great smile, a sense of humor and I have to say the woman was built thick for an Asian chick. I loved the way her kimono style dress clung in all the right spots. The way the slit on the side showed almost all of her thigh. Her breasts were heavy and her ass was high and round like a black chick.

Usually I don't get a second glance from anyone other than black women or the occasional white girl looking to try something a little darker and a little different. I was surprised the day I went in to grab take out and Sue Ling gave me a wink. The Dragon had been my favorite spot ever since

"How are you tonight Su Ling? As always, you know just what I want." I said, flashing my most tempting smile and running my hands over my dreds.

"We are closing soon, so it may be a few extra minutes if you do not mind waiting. Sit in the dining area, it is much cooler back there."

I thanked her, grabbed a newspaper and headed to the back dining area. To my surprise it was a completely empty. Most of the staff must have already cleared out for the evening. There wasn't even enough light for me to read my paper. The room was very comfy with red carpet and candle light from the tables playing across the dragon ornaments on the wall. I kicked my feet up on the chair across from me and leaned my head back. I must have dozed off for a minute because when I opened my eyes I could no longer hear any clanging from the kitchen. A glance at my watch showed that I had been here for twenty minutes. I looked to my left and there was Su Ling, a beer in one hand and a plastic bag in the other.

She smiled at me in such an alluring way that I had to do a double take. She laughed and handed me the beer as she sat across from me, putting the plastic bag on the seat beside her. I took a gulp, it was icy cold and felt good going down after a long day at work. I thanked her and sat watching her watch me drink my beer. I can't lie, I was enjoying letting my eyes roam her up and down, lingering for just a brief moment on the tightness of her dress across her nipples. However I couldn't help but wonder why she was holding my food hostage.

"I don't want to hold you up if you need to finish closing up, I know your brothers wait for you after they close the kitchen." I said, finally met her eyes.

Leaning in she said, "Trey, everyone has already left. Father had to go home early tonight and I told my brothers that you and I were going to see a late movie and then you would bring me home. They are very happy that I am beginning to make more American friends. Female friends especially. They are very untrusting of young men wanting to spend time with me."

"Oh no", I thought. She has already thrown me into that friend category. She thinks I am straight and we are going to be bffs or some girly shit like that.

"Well, I hadn't really planned on seeing a movie tonight, but since your brothers have already left I can give you a ride home." I needed to try and get myself out of this situation that was going totally in a different direction then I had planned. I had enough friends, that is not what I was looking for at this point. Maybe it was the cultural differences that had me believing she was feelin me. I guess I must have misread those signals.

Su Ling stood up and walked across to the bar and grabbed another beer, slowly popping off the cap as she walked back to our table. She took a long sip then sat the bottle down in front of me. "Silly Trey, that is just what I told them so that I could get you alone for once."

Su Ling bent her head, grabbed my dreds and gave me the most mouthwatering kiss I'd ever had. She tasted like summer and smelled like orchids. As I slid my hands over the silky smooth kimono down her hips and around to her ass, she moaned and leaned in closer. My heart started to pound like a drum in my chest as she stood and turned around so that I could unzip her dress. Once she pulled her arms out of the dress it slid down her body as if in slow motion, fluttering to the floor to pool around her feet. I stood and held her hand as she stepped out of the dress. She was wearing a black bra, black panties ... and a black garter. I was surprised but not disappointed. I pulled the chopstick like hair pin that was holding her hair in place, leaving it to tumble in soft waves down her neck.

Before I could even get the "*damn*", out of my mouth she kissed me. It was rough and tinged with excitement. She pressed her full body against me. I grabbed her ass and she moaned louder. Slowly I ran my hand down her plump ass, around to her hip and traced my fingers up the already damp "v" of her black panties. She was already so wet. I could feel my own body responding, feeling the subtle slickness between my thighs. All I could think was "*fuck, this chick is hot.*"

She pulled away, giving me a wink as she took off her bra and did a sexy shimmy out of her panties. I stood there with my mouth practically hanging open as Su Ling rubbed one hand over her already hard nipples and down her stomach. "Trey, do you like?" she said as she slowly raised one foot onto the chair beside her so that I could get a good look as she moved her hand down lower to stroke her clit.

I reached for my beer and finished it in one gulp. "Hell yeah I like!"

Quickly I took off my work shirt so that I now stood in my jeans and beater. My tits are small so I never bother with a bra. Why be uncomfortable if you don't have to. The cool air conditioning immediately made my own nipples stand at attention. I could see that Su Ling noticed this, because she stopped her show and eyed me up and down. She started to take her foot off the chair.

"No." I said, moving closer to her. "Stay just like that." I stepped closer using my best bad boi swagger. Bending my head I sucked her small nipple and ran my own hand over the now glistening line separating her lips. She sighed as I touched her and arched into me, forcing her nipple deeper into my mouth. Gently I parted her lips and slid my finger against the wetness. I placed my other hand on the small of her back to steady her as she began to rock against my hand. Slowly I entered her with one finger to test how much she could take. She was tight but not so much that I couldn't add another finger without causing her any discomfort.

She started to moan again and began rocking her hips faster. Hell just her tightness around my fingers was making my own pussy clench with want.

"Fuck me Trey, fuck me hard." She whispered against my ear. I heard a low growl rumble from my chest. I slid deeper into to her pumping my fingers in and out. In and out, stroking her now hardening clit with my thumb on every inward stroke. Su Ling was squeezing my shoulder so hard I knew I would be bruised in the morning. She was starting to shake and I knew she was close. I pulled out one final time. Grabbing her around the waist, I picked her up and laid her on the dragon embroidered table cloth on the table beside us.

"Spread your legs for me baby." I said, as I took off my beater and balled it up to place under her hips for a better angle. She licked her lips and did as she was told. I parted her lips with my thumbs and traced my name across her clit with my tongue. When I got to the "y" she started to buck

68

hard against my face. I firmly held her thighs and pushed my tongue inside her tightness. She was soo sweet. I moved my tongue in and out, repeating the same moves my fingers had played earlier. I could feel her wetness running down my chin and it just made me want more. Slowly I dragged my tongue over her clit, licking circles while she withered beneath me. I felt her body begin to shake again and her back arched off the table. I added a little more pressure and she screamed my name and tightened her thighs around my neck. I was lost in the zone. Nothing existed but the scent and taste of her. I did another sweep of her clit from bottom to top. Her grip on my head got tighter and I felt her whole body go rigid as she yelled out something in Chinese. She lay back on the table panting as I rested my head on her thigh.

"Trey. Trey, that was unbelievable." She purred as she sat up. I took her hand to help her off the table. I reached for a napkin to wipe my mouth. She put her hand over mine, stopping me, and licked her juices from my chin and lips before slipping her tongue into my mouth. Then she gave my nipple a tweak, causing me to moan. She smiled, "It is getting late, my father will be waiting up for me." She was still naked as she lifted the plastic bag that was still sitting on the chair. Guessing that was my cue that she was done with me, I looked around to find my shirt and beater so that I could get dressed. Su Ling shook the bag. "Trey are you still feeling hungry?" She said with a sly smile on her face.

"Um, actually I am starving." I reached for the bag and she shook her head no.

"Sorry Trey, I must have forgotten to put your order in. This is my bag but I will share with you if you like." Su Ling reached in the bag and pulled out a purple dildo. For the second time tonight, my jaw dropped nearly to the floor. For a second I was totally speechless. What did she think she was going to do with that? Don't get me wrong, I have been fucked before, but I don't make a habit of letting every chick in town do it. I'm just not that kind of dyke. "What is wrong Trey? Cat got your tongue? That is what is wrong with you Americans. You think all Chinese women are innocent little Geisha dolls. She reached into the bag and pulled out a tube of KY, the kind that heats up. Su Ling rubbed my breast and then squeezed my nipple again causing me to suck in my breath. "I will only ask once more. Are you still hungry Trey?" She looked me in the eyes as she ran the dildo up the side of my leg.

I thought about it for a second. *Hell it's not like she is one of the girls from the factory or even the club. Who is she going to tell?*

"Yeah babe, starving." I said, reaching to unbuckle my belt.

I guess I will be stopping for overpriced pizza on the way home.

* Originally published in Bad Girl Tales (Waid Books, 2014)

Don't Get It Twisted

There seems to be
some misconception
about the way I
choose to spread my
affection
around

and to whom I offer my
attention

I may be soft-spoken
but don't get it twisted
I'm nobody's bitch

My love making is gifted and
I pack a big stick

I offer more variety then
your man ever could
White, Black, Asian, pink if you choose

Silicon, rubber,
even the stroke of my glass dildo
you will find is nice
I handle them all with more finesse then
LL rocks a mic

Let me make it clear

so that you will be sure to understand

Yes, I 'm that dyke in the office,
that dyke down town
I'm that dyke that keeps your girl company
when you ain't around

Now that it's been said,
I hope get the gist
I hope you understand
because trust and believe
your auntie, your sister, even your mother
might be found on my list

About Us...

Neia Bailey, also known as *Purpose*, is the definition of both brains and beauty with a degree in marketing and a penchant for pole dancing. A member of Harrisburg's premier spoken word collective, I Am Words, Neia is an accomplished spoken word performer who still resides in her Harrisburg hometown.

Denise Cherubini was born and raised in the ghettos of Connecticut and lived above the Hell's Angels Club House in Bridgeport. She won awards to study Fine Art and Creative Writing at the Arts at Wesleyan University's C.C.Y, The Educational Center for Art in New Haven, CT and Maryland Institute College of Art. She has been a featured artist and spoken word performer from New York City to Baltimore, MD to Washington D.C.. Her poetry and illustrations have been in various publications and his beat poetry manuscript "Heartbeat" was nominated for a Baltimore Artscape Literary Award in 1998. Most recently, she formed the Trans* spectrum conceptual performance art bandTransexual Fetus. She also founded theTrans Baltimore Outreach Society - TBOS, a Baltimore inner city Trans* outreach program offering free counseling to Trans* people. Denise, at the time of the writing of these pieces, is now Devin and continues to live his dynamic life of art and activism in Baltimore.

Jacki King is a saucy Southern comedy writer who wants to sex you up. Since winning the Amber Heat competition with the erotic short story "She Who Laughs Last" in 2005, Jacki King has been sharing stories with sizzle and sass; after all, what's more entertaining than what two people will do to get into one another's pants (or hearts)? Her releases include the paperback collection *Jacki's Jewels* (available online via Amazon, Barnes and Noble or AmberHeat.com). She currently lives in Central PA where she writes, lectures, teaches, loves, and laughs. You can reach her on Facebook or on Twitter @ReadJackiKing.

For *Mocha Moma*, also known as Khianna Palmer, writing poetry started at the early age of six when she received her first journal. From there, her writing developed a love for words and rhymes that lead to performing poetry and songs as the years went by. At the age of 10 she moved from Indiana with her family to Pennsylvania and drifted away from her writing. It wasn't until 15 years later that she decided to pick up the pen and pad again, but this time it wasn't because she wanted to say something, it was because she had something to say. Giving birth to her passion gave her the power to empower. After writing for two publishing companies since 2011, Mocha Moma was honored to join I Am Words in their movement to make a difference through words. When she isn't writing articles, poetry, or performing she enjoys volunteering, playing sports, and above all, family time.

Maria James-Thiaw is the author of three poetry collections: *Windows to the Soul* (Shippensburg University Press, 1999), *Rising Waters* (Shippensburg University Press, 2003) and her latest, *Talking "White"* (PostDada Press, 2013) In 2006, she produced an independent CD of spoken word and music entitled *FREEverse*. Her poetry has been published in a variety of journals including *Black Magnolias, Fledgling Rag,* and *One Trick Pony Review.* She is a professor of literary and cultural studies at Central Penn College where she founded the Knight Writers creative writing club and co-edits an online student literary journal called The Central Pen. She holds a Master's degree in Communications Studies from Shippensburg University (2003) and a Masters of Fine Arts in Creative Writing from Goddard College (2009.)

The Priestess. the performance name for Carla Christopher-Waid, is a former social worker and teacher turned artist and a former dancer and actress turned poet. She runs PoemSugar Press, writes books of her own and does a lot of other stuff that can be found at carlachristopher.com.

T.L. Waid is the author of *Something Sensual* (Waid Books, 2012) and *Love and Other Misunderstandings* (Waid Books, 2011). She is also the brains behind Waid Book which you can learn more about at waidbooks.com.

With Gratitude...

The ladies of *Below the Belt* would like to thank:

Our respective significant others, children, families and friends who have shown us endless support and patience during this project.

The staff of G's Jook Joint, Charm City Kitty Club, The Almost Uptown Poetry Cartel, The Southcentral Pennsylvania LGBT Center and all our friends from the tour.

The inventor of the Hurricane Margarita.

You! Thank you for purchasing, reading and hopefully thoroughly enjoying this delicious collection!

For information on *Below the Belt* tour dates and authors or to learn about forthcoming books in the Below the Belt Series log onto:

http://www.facebook.com/belowthebelt
http://www.facebook.com/poemsugar
http://www.poemsugarpress.com

Other books available
in the Below the Belt series from
PoemSugar Press...

Below the Belt (2013)
Below the Belt 2; Go Lower (2014)
Below the Belt 3; Suck-her Punch! (2015)
Below the Belt - Men; Come Harder (2015)

Available at poemsugarpress.com
and on Amazon

www.ingramcontent.com/pod-product-compliance
Lightning Source LLC
Chambersburg PA
CBHW070608180626
46817CB00005B/2048